For Megan Schlueter   E.J.

For my sister, Maureen   K.O.

Text copyright © 1994 by Ellen Jackson
Illustrations copyright © 1994 by Kevin O'Malley

should be addressed to Lothrop, Lee & Shepard Books, a division of William Morrow & Company, Inc.,
1350 Avenue of the Americas, New York, New York 10019.
Printed in the United States of America

First Edition   1   2   3   4   5   6   7   8   9   10
Library of Congress Cataloging in Publication
Jackson, Ellen B., Cinder Edna / Ellen Jackson ; illustrated by Kevin O'Malley.
p.   cm.   Summary: Cinderella and Cinder Edna, who live with cruel stepmothers and
stepsisters, have different approaches to life; and, although each ends up with the prince of her
dreams, one is a great deal happier than the other. ISBN 0-688-12322-8. — ISBN 0-688-12323-6
(lib. bdg.)   [1. Fairy tales.]   I. O'Malley, Kevin, ill.   II. Title.   PZ8.J17Ci   1994
[E]—dc20   92-44160   CIP   AC

Cinder Edna

BY ELLEN JACKSON
ILLUSTRATED BY KEVIN O'MALLEY

LOTHROP, LEE & SHEPARD BOOKS
NEW YORK

Once upon a time there were two girls who lived next door to each other. You may have heard of the first one. Her name was Cinderella. Poor Cinderella was forced to work from morning till night, cooking and scrubbing pots and pans and picking up after her cruel stepmother and wicked stepsisters. When her work was done, she sat among the cinders to keep warm, thinking about all her troubles.

$\mathcal{C}$inder Edna, the other girl, was also forced to work for her wicked stepmother and stepsisters. But she sang and whistled while she worked. Moreover, she had learned a thing or two from doing all that housework—such as how to make tuna casserole sixteen different ways and how to get spots off everything from rugs to ladybugs.

Edna had tried sitting in the cinders a few times.
But it seemed like a silly way to spend time. Besides, it
just made her clothes black and sooty. Instead when
the housework was done, she kept warm by mowing
the lawn and cleaning parrot cages for the neighbors
at $1.50 an hour. She also taught herself to play
the accordion.

Even with her ragged, sooty clothing Cinderella
was quite beautiful.

Edna, on the other hand, wasn't much to look at.
But she was strong and spunky and knew some good
jokes—including an especially funny one about an
anteater from Afghanistan.

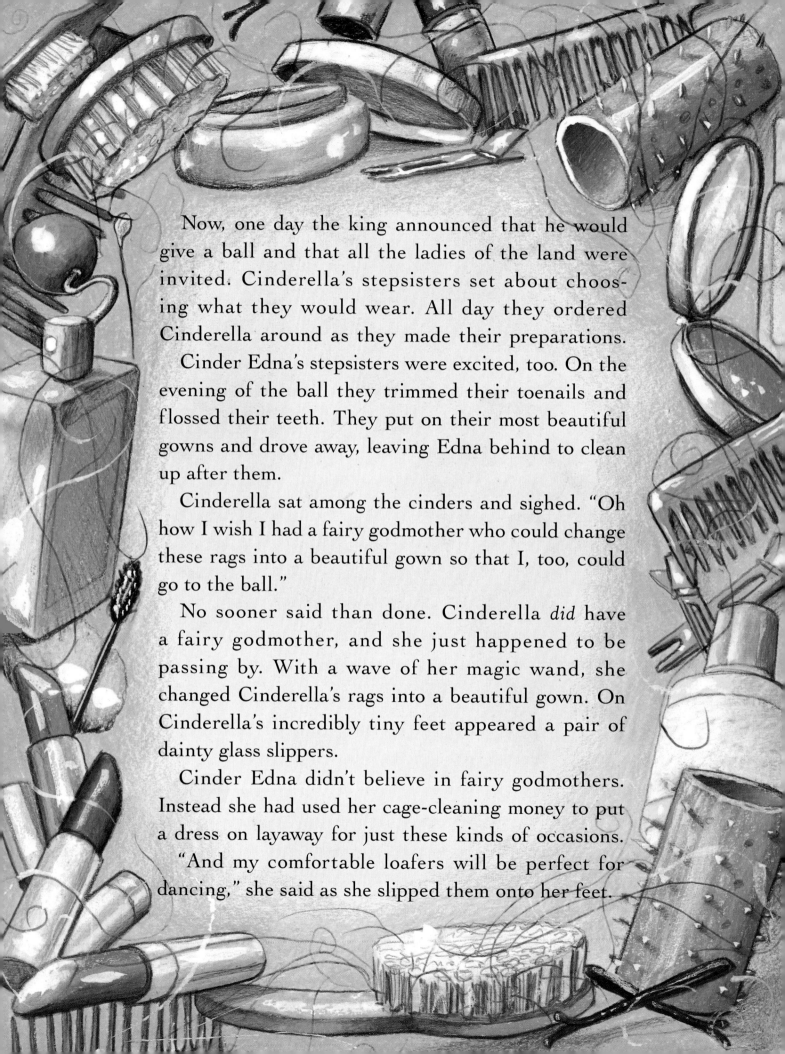

Now, one day the king announced that he would give a ball and that all the ladies of the land were invited. Cinderella's stepsisters set about choosing what they would wear. All day they ordered Cinderella around as they made their preparations.

Cinder Edna's stepsisters were excited, too. On the evening of the ball they trimmed their toenails and flossed their teeth. They put on their most beautiful gowns and drove away, leaving Edna behind to clean up after them.

Cinderella sat among the cinders and sighed. "Oh how I wish I had a fairy godmother who could change these rags into a beautiful gown so that I, too, could go to the ball."

No sooner said than done. Cinderella *did* have a fairy godmother, and she just happened to be passing by. With a wave of her magic wand, she changed Cinderella's rags into a beautiful gown. On Cinderella's incredibly tiny feet appeared a pair of dainty glass slippers.

Cinder Edna didn't believe in fairy godmothers. Instead she had used her cage-cleaning money to put a dress on layaway for just these kinds of occasions.

"And my comfortable loafers will be perfect for dancing," she said as she slipped them onto her feet.

Meanwhile Cinderella's big, bright eyes brimmed with tears. "But, Fairy Godmother, how will I get to the ball?"

The fairy godmother was surprised that her god-daughter couldn't seem to figure anything out for herself. However, with another wave of the wand, she changed a pumpkin into a carriage, six white mice into horses, and a stray rat into a coachman.

"Be sure to leave before midnight," she warned Cinderella as she helped her into the elegant carriage.

Cinder Edna took the bus.

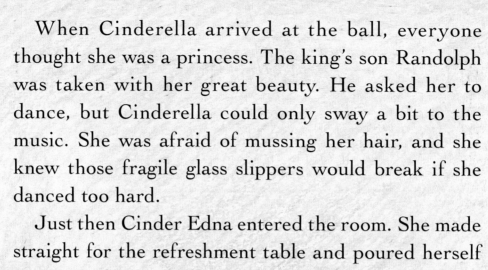

When Cinderella arrived at the ball, everyone thought she was a princess. The king's son Randolph was taken with her great beauty. He asked her to dance, but Cinderella could only sway a bit to the music. She was afraid of mussing her hair, and she knew those fragile glass slippers would break if she danced too hard.

Just then Cinder Edna entered the room. She made straight for the refreshment table and poured herself some punch. It was Randolph's princely duty to greet everyone, so he came over to say hello.

"What's it like, being a prince?" Edna asked, to make conversation.

"Quite fantastic," said the prince. "Mostly I review the troops and sit around on the throne looking brave and wise." He turned his head so that Edna could see how handsome his chin looked from the right side.

"Borrring," thought Edna.

"Excuse me, but we recycle plastic around here," said a little man with glasses and a warm smile.

"Just ignore him," said Randolph. "He's only my younger brother, Rupert. He lives in a cottage in the back and runs the recycling plant and a home for orphaned kittens."

Cinder Edna immediately handed Rupert her cup.

"Would you like to dance?" asked Rupert.

Cinder Edna and Rupert danced and danced. They did the Storybook Stomp and the Cinnamon Twist. They did the Worm and the Fish. They boogied and woogied. At last they stopped for a round of punch. Edna learned that Rupert (1) loved tuna casserole, (2) played the concertina, (3) knew some good jokes.

She told him the one about the anteater from Afghanistan and he told her the one about the banana from Barbados.

They were deep in a conversation about gum wrappers and rusty tin cans when the clock began to strike twelve.

"Oh," cried Cinderella, running for the door. "The magic spell disappears at midnight."

"Oh, oh," cried Cinder Edna, running for the door. "The buses stop running at midnight!"

Randolph and Rupert ran after the two girls.

"Wait! Wait!" they called. But it was too late.

As the girls vanished into the night, the two princes ran smack-dab into each other on the palace steps.

Whap! They landed with a thud. Rupert's glasses went flying and broke into a million pieces on the cement.

"Look what you made me do!" said Randolph. "Now she's gone—the only girl I ever loved."

"Well, didn't you get her name?" asked Rupert impatiently. "The one I love is named Edna."

"Gee, I forgot to ask," said Randolph, scratching his head.

As Rupert got up he stumbled over something. When he leaned close to look, he saw two shoes lying side by side on the steps. One was a scuffed-up loafer. The other was a dainty glass slipper. "These definitely should be recycled," he said.

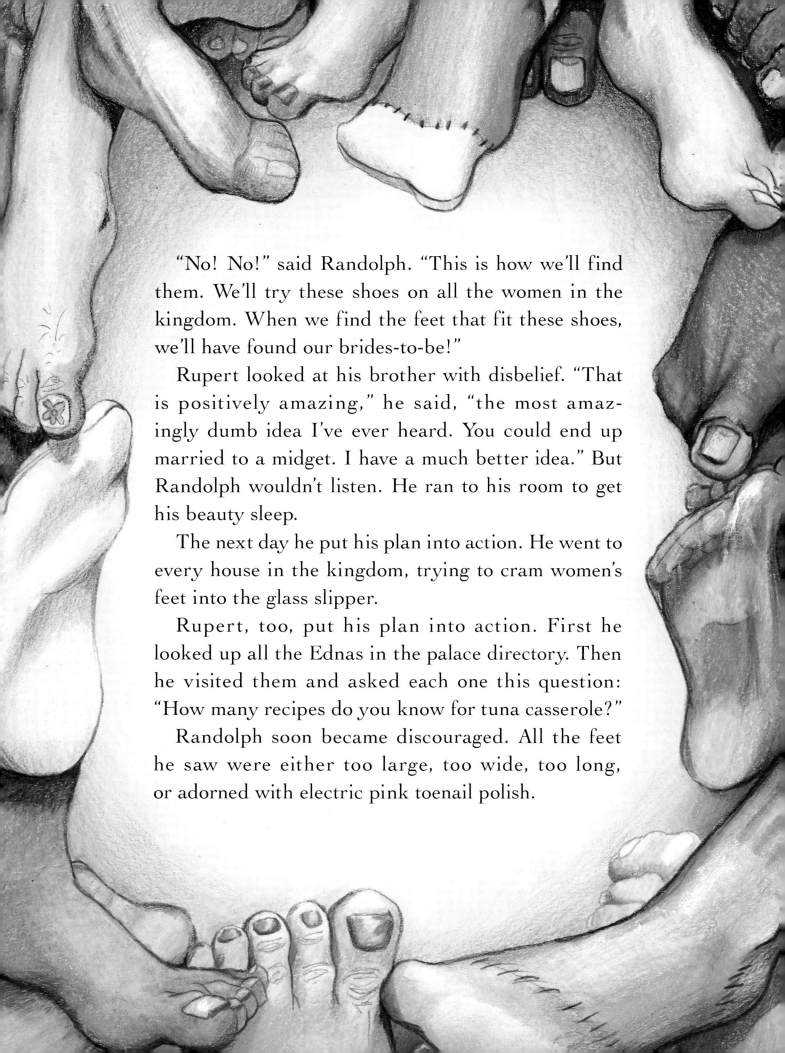

"No! No!" said Randolph. "This is how we'll find them. We'll try these shoes on all the women in the kingdom. When we find the feet that fit these shoes, we'll have found our brides-to-be!"

Rupert looked at his brother with disbelief. "That is positively amazing," he said, "the most amazingly dumb idea I've ever heard. You could end up married to a midget. I have a much better idea." But Randolph wouldn't listen. He ran to his room to get his beauty sleep.

The next day he put his plan into action. He went to every house in the kingdom, trying to cram women's feet into the glass slipper.

Rupert, too, put his plan into action. First he looked up all the Ednas in the palace directory. Then he visited them and asked each one this question: "How many recipes do you know for tuna casserole?"

Randolph soon became discouraged. All the feet he saw were either too large, too wide, too long, or adorned with electric pink toenail polish.

Rupert, too, was discouraged. While some Ednas could name tuna casserole with pecan sauce, and others could name tuna casserole with sour cream and rice, no one could name more than seven kinds of tuna casserole.

Finally Randolph got to Cinderella's house. The cruel stepsisters were eager to try on the glass slipper, but, of course, it didn't fit either of them.

Suddenly Randolph noticed a woman in rags, sitting forlornly among the cinders in the corner. Something about her seemed familiar.

"Oh, Miss. Why don't you try this on?" he suggested. With trembling hands, Cinderella tried on the glass slipper. It fit perfectly!

Randolph swept her up in his arms and carried her
away to the palace so that they could be married.

Meanwhile Rupert reached Cinder Edna's house. Her wicked stepsisters wanted to try on the loafer, but Rupert wouldn't let them because they weren't named Edna.

At that moment, Cinder Edna came in from mowing the lawn. Her heart almost stopped when she saw Rupert. He blinked nearsightedly at her.

Without his glasses Cinder Edna looked something
like a large plate of mashed potatoes.

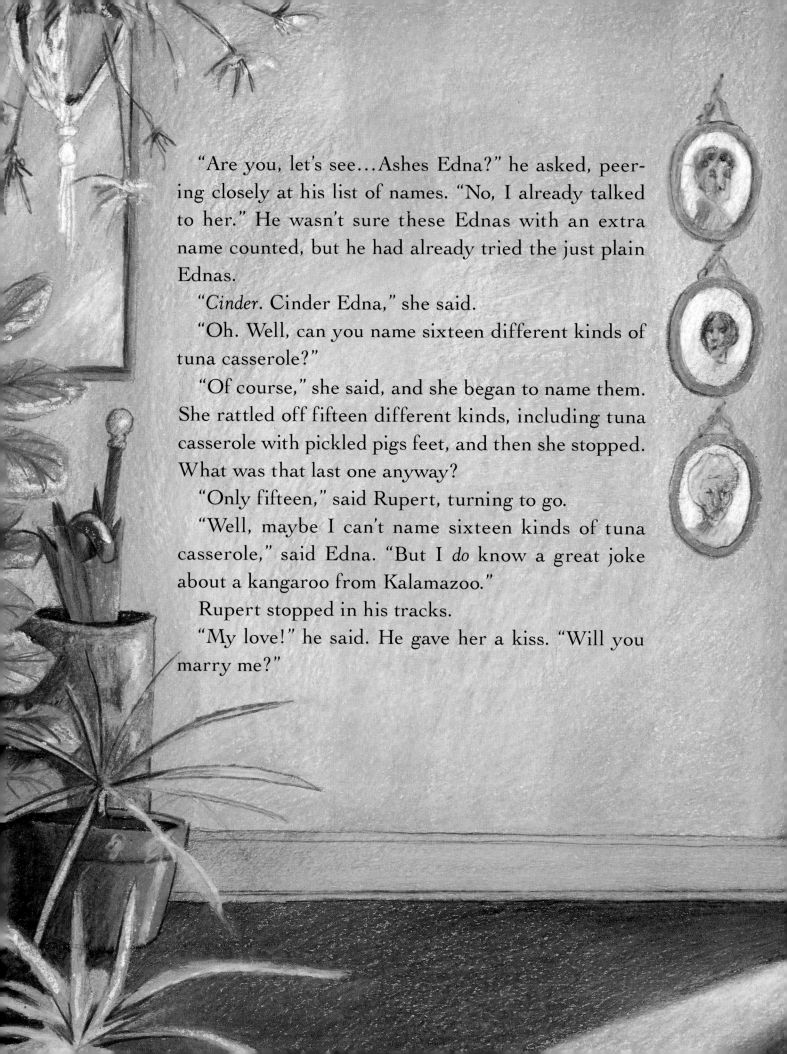

"Are you, let's see…Ashes Edna?" he asked, peering closely at his list of names. "No, I already talked to her." He wasn't sure these Ednas with an extra name counted, but he had already tried the just plain Ednas.

"*Cinder*. Cinder Edna," she said.

"Oh. Well, can you name sixteen different kinds of tuna casserole?"

"Of course," she said, and she began to name them. She rattled off fifteen different kinds, including tuna casserole with pickled pigs feet, and then she stopped. What was that last one anyway?

"Only fifteen," said Rupert, turning to go.

"Well, maybe I can't name sixteen kinds of tuna casserole," said Edna. "But I *do* know a great joke about a kangaroo from Kalamazoo."

Rupert stopped in his tracks.

"My love!" he said. He gave her a kiss. "Will you marry me?"

Soon after that, Randolph and Ella (she dropped the cinder part) and Rupert and Edna (she did the same) were married in a grand double ceremony.

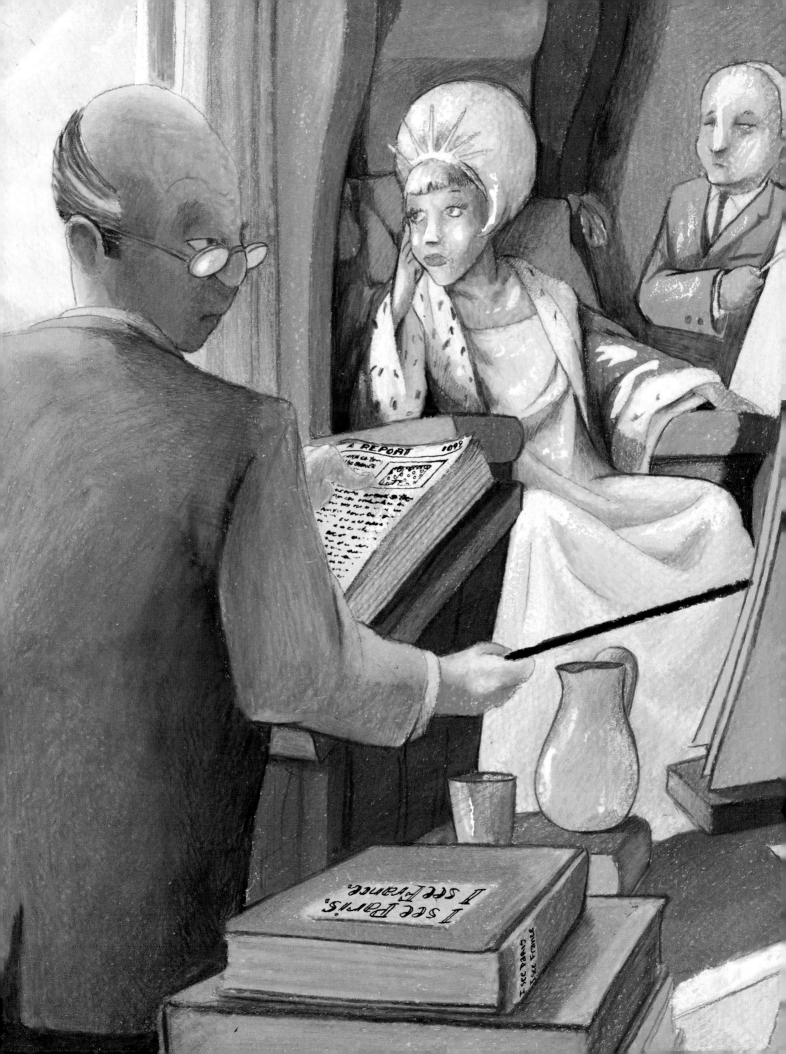

So the girl who had once been known as Cinderella ended up in a big palace. During the day she went to endless ceremonies and listened to dozens of speeches by His Highness the Grand Archduke of Lethargia and the Second Deputy Underassistant of Underwear. And at night she sat by the fire with nothing to look at but her husband's perfect profile while he talked endlessly of troops, parade formations, and uniform buttons.

And the girl who had been known as Cinder Edna ended up in a small cottage with solar heating. During the day she studied waste disposal engineering and cared for orphaned kittens. And at night she and her husband laughed and joked, tried new recipes together, and played duets on the accordion and concertina.

Guess who lived happily ever after.